Published in the United States by Crown Publishers, Inc.,
225 Park Avenue South, New York, New York 10003.
Published in Great Britain by Walker Books Ltd.,
184-192 Drummond Street, London NW1 3HP
CROWN is a trademark of Crown Publishers, Inc.
Manufactured in Italy

Library of Congress Cataloging-in-Publication Data
Carter, Anne.
Scurry's treasure.
(It's great to read!)
Summary: Scurry the red squirrel and his friend Fly find nuts to
bury for the winter, but discover one of them isn't a real nut
at all.
[1. Squirrels—Fiction] I. Butler, John, Ill,. II. Title. III. Series.
PZ7.C2427Sc 1987 [E] 86-24260
ISBN 0-517-56535-8

10 9 8 7 6 5 4 3 2 1

First Edition

IT'S GREAT TO READ!™

SCURRY'S TREASURE

Written by ANNE CARTER
Illustrated by JOHN BUTLER

CROWN PUBLISHERS, INC., NEW YORK

Scurry, the red squirrel, lived in Mrs. Pym's garden. He didn't know it was her garden. He thought it was his own.

He liked to sit in the tall beech tree, eating beechnuts in the sun.

Scurry shared the garden with his friend Fly.

They played games up and down the tree trunks and chased each other over the lawn.

Whenever people came out of the house, Scurry and Fly ran up the tree and froze. They lay so still, they were sure no one could see them.

When the people went away there were often things to eat left on the grass: crumbly cake and bits of apple and nuts to bury for the winter.

If there was orange, Scurry and Fly left it. They didn't like it.

One day, Scurry found a beautiful hazelnut. He was going to bury it near the cedar tree, but one of the people kept walking close by. He chattered at her, wanting her to go away. At last she did.

Scurry finished burying his nut.
Then he found another one.
It was big and smooth and very
shiny, not like a hazelnut at all.

Scurry buried this one, too.

Winter came. The days were short and cold. Scurry and Fly slept a lot, curled up in their cedar tree home. When they woke up, they were hungry.

There were no crumbs under the tree. Scurry smelled nuts. He dug one up. Near it was another. It was the very shiny nut he had buried weeks before.

Fly was watching. She ran up and snatched it.

Scurry chased her and she ran up a tree. Fly held the nut in her paws and tried to crack it with her teeth. But the nut was too hard. It hurt Fly's teeth. She dropped it.

"Grandma! Look what the squirrels have found!"

One of the small people had come out of the house. Scurry saw her pick up his shiny nut.

"The stone out of your brooch. The one you lost!"

"Clever little squirrels! Let's give them a present in return. They must be hungry."

Something round and brown bounced and rolled on the grass. Scurry chased after it. He held it in his paws and bit the soft brown shell. Inside, he found a nut.

Fly was there when the next one landed.

Two hungry squirrels shared their unusual feast of chocolate-covered nuts!

Next time they woke, winter was almost over and there were lots of new green buds to eat.